Bloodgrue
Volume 4: Attractions

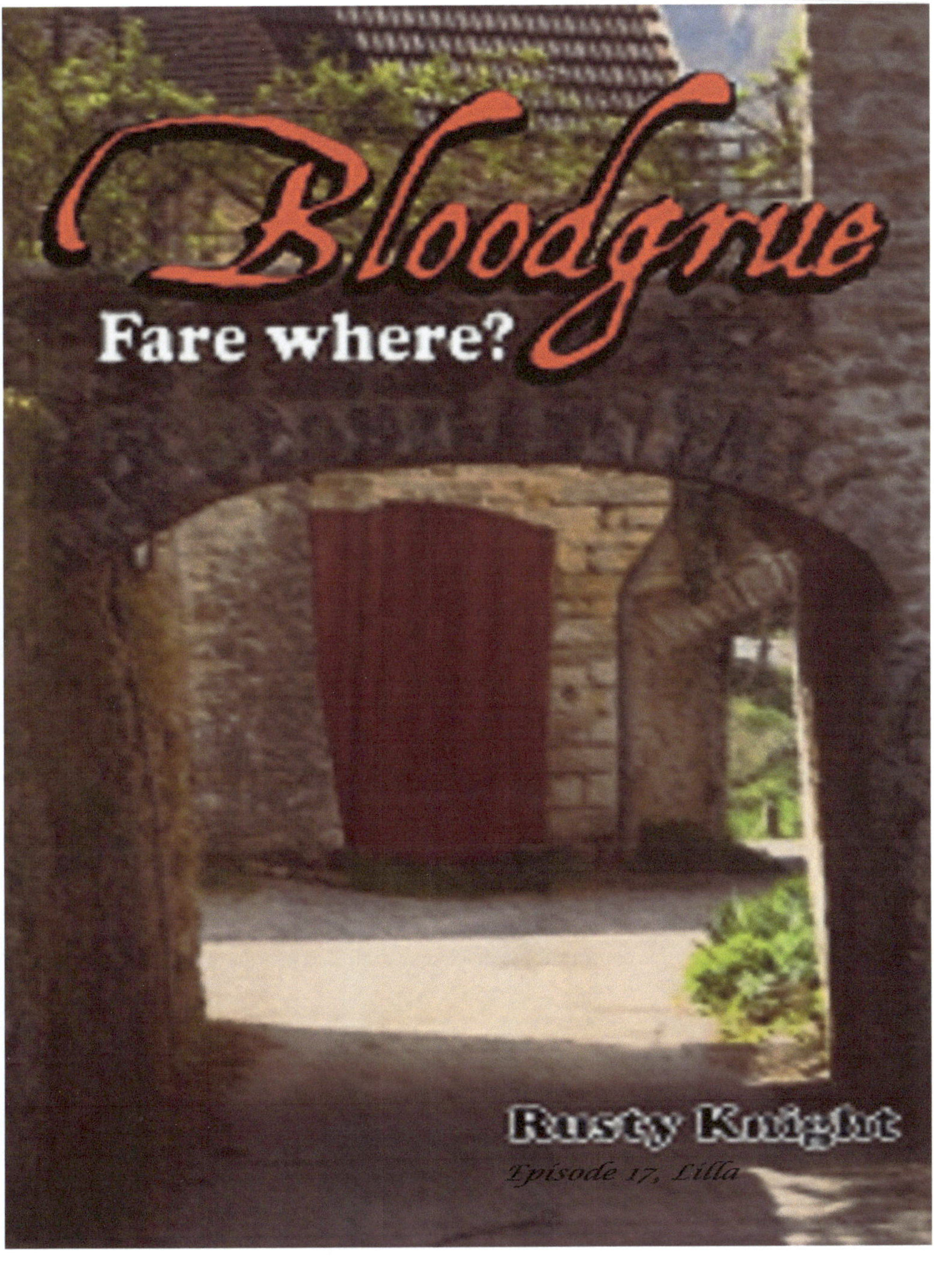
Bloodgrue
Fare where?
Rusty Knight
Episode 17, Lilla

Welcome to our serial stories!

If you're not familiar with our serials, think of them as a favorite nighttime program that continues with a new episode each week, only this is in a print format. These are stories that don't necessarily have an end planned for them, or if they do, it's a long way off unlike many television series that we get interested in, only to have them go off air.

Serial stories are a great way to keep you entertained and on edge waiting to see what will happen next, in short enough episodes to enjoy on a lunch break, or before going to bed. Although our stories are designed to be read one episode per week, unlike TV stories, if you just can't wait for the next episode, you can get another one any time.

Be sure to download when you purchase!

It is a good idea to download the episode when you first purchase them. Then, read them at your leisure.

Please feel free to let us know what you think of our serial stories. It's a trend and that may take some getting used to, but we've had positive feedback in the past with them.

Now, it's time to enjoy!

From Rusty Knight & InUPress, Thank you

We would like to acknowledge the following for their work in the production of this series.

Our cover design is by, C S Burgar

All of our editing is by, Donna Shumaker (Aria)

Bloodgrue
Volume 4: Attractions

As producer at InUPress.ca and author of the Bloodgrue serial short-story series, I thank you for reading Bloodgrue Volume 4: Attractions by Rusty Knight.

The series will be continued with Bloodgrue Volume 5: Rulings

These will be found at InUPress.ca and Amazon and Kobo

Previous books in the series are now available at Amazon:

Bloodgrue Volume 1: Fare Where!

Bloodgrue Volume 2: Breaths

Bloodgrue Volume 3: Business also available on Kobo and InUPress.ca

Bloodgrue Volume 4: Attractions also available on InUPress and Kobo

As producer at InUPress.ca and author of the Bloodgrue, Markus and Lanis serial short-story series I thank you for reading our series.

Yours,
Rusty Knight and InUPress.ca.

Dalan e-zine can also can be found on InUPress.ca and other works can be found at such places as InUPress.ca, Amazon, Kobo, Goodreads, Niume and Scriggler.

Books in the Bloodgrue series now available at www.inupress.ca, Kindle, Kobo and as well on Amazon in paperback:

Bloodgrue Volume 1: Fare Where? Amazon and Kindle only

Bloodgrue Volume 2: Breaths Amazon and Kindle only

Bloodgrue Volume 3: Business

Bloodgrue Volume 4: Attractions

Previously on *Bloodgrue **Spring 65 Raccoon***,

    Bloodgrue was summoned by Ottar Marrel for a run for his customer Mel. On the journey Bloodgrue dealt with beggar Andolf again, and then with a thief named Annelee. Developing a rapport with Annelee, Bloodgrue offered her a rescue job with Luenen. In the run back to Ottar, Bloodgrue won a bet and earned two Flairs. Bloodgrue hatched, in the process of the journey, a plan to deal with Andolf.

Bloodgrue
By Rusty Knight
Episode seventeen, 'Lilla'

In U Press

Inevitable Unicorn Press

We continue on …

Summer 1 Raccoon,

Bloodgrue sits up in his bed. Scratching from the wool blanket against his skin, he is annoyed. Getting up and using the chamber pot, Bloodgrue plans his day.

With all his morning chores complete, Bloodgrue walks along Willow Road then Osmo Road. Bloodgrue turns south-west going along Elmar Road until he enters Teptun's Square and Market from the east. Bloodgrue contemplates what his goal is, coin wise, before he will be heading home.

He walks the alleys between the stalls and shops, watching people for tells of possible clients. As Bloodgrue is crossing an intersection in the north, near the fountain, a beautiful jalfem of about twenty years of age, hails Bloodgrue eagerly. "Gods-grace and good fate dragoman how do you fare?

Bloodgrue smiles while pondering the event. Though this is not the stunning beauty who he is seeking, this is a possible client who is very pleasing to his eyes. "Gods-grace and good fate master. I am well. How do you fare? How may I be of service?"

The young woman grins happily. "Yes … yes you can be of service. I am well thank you. I am to understand you are an honest dragoman for hire who is strong and knows North Docks very well. I need your services for many runs delivering my goods. Today I need to deliver six crates. Are you available?"

Bloodgrue, noticing she mentioned many runs, sees a future client here. So he nods. "Yes I am available today. Where are we going?"

Beaming an even larger grin, the woman offers her arm to clasp. "I am journeyman brick-maker and potter Lilla. I mostly do pottery, but I make bricks as well. My shop is where we are going right now. Follow me to my shop and we will load my cart, then you will help me find my customer for my delivery. How much do you charge dragoman?"

Bloodgrue nods while smiling. "I am Apprentice Dragoman Bloodgrue of 4212 Willow Road. My fees are one Dyns a day, or two dusters per kilometre. Do you have a name or address for your customer who we are delivering to today?"

Lilla smiles, "Yes, it's called the Low Bilge tavern. Do you know it?"

Bloodgrue smiles cheerfully. "Yes I do … it is down in Low Tide ward. It will take about five or six hours to get to. We should be able to get there today. What address is your shop?"

Lilla starts walking west towards Spider Avenue. She says heartily "I work from 3086 Spider Avenue. Do you know it?"

Bloodgrue ponders it briefly. He has been down Spider Avenue a few times. "Yes … I know the shop. It is a small two story wood and stone structure on the south side of the avenue."

Lilla shifts around to look at Bloodgrue and speaks rapidly. "Old Blue Hair was right. You know the area well. Come on, let's go slow poke. It's about a kilometre from the market."

They arrive at the shop about half an hour after noon. Lilla insists on preparing a lunch while Bloodgrue loads her cart.

Looking at the lunch, Bloodgrue ponders this; cold pickled fish fillet and pickled carrots, with hot cooked rice spiced with pepper and lemon grass. Bloodgrue rarely eats this well at home for a regular meal. Using the etiquette taught to him by Ottar, Bloodgrue begins the meal with Lilla.

"How long have you been a journeyman Lilla?" asks a politely curious Bloodgrue.

Lilla smirks proudly. "Two years. I passed my journeyman tests Spring 10, two years ago. Master Fells sponsored me my last year, as my journeyman brick-maker passed away from blood-fires when I was sixteen. She cut herself and blood-fires set in and three days later she passed away. This was her shop. I bought it with a loan from Master Fells, which I am paying off quickly. It is almost paid off … in less than half the time I was supposed to pay it off in."

Bloodgrue is impressed by this and replies. "So you became a journeyman two years ago, convinced your sponsor to loan you the funds to purchase this shop and in the two years since you've paid off half the loan already … in less than half the time agreed to on the loan? Very impressive … I have been an apprentice dragoman for over five years and my master refuses to sponsor my journeyman testing. He just recently started teaching me more than the routes of North Docks. Everything I have, I acquired outside of working for my master. I think I might be very impressed with you Lilla."

Bloodgrue finishes eating the last morsel of edible food Lilla offered him. All that remains on the plate are the fish bones. His ale mug is empty as well. He wipes his hands and face with the cloth provided by Lilla.

Bloodgrue then stands. "I'm ready to hit the street after I help you with the dishes Lilla."

Lila laughs like a flowing stream and then responds. "Leave the dishes; I will look after them later. We need to get these mugs and plates to the Low Bilge today. That was my promise to Lennie the tavern keeper."

Together they set out. Bloodgrue pulls the hand cart while Lilla walks beside him holding a conversation.

Walking along Spider Avenue, Bloodgrue leads back out to Teptun's Square and Market. Then north through the main alley, up to the north exit onto Elmar Road and out to Osmo Road, then they walk to Low Tide ward and Water Way Street.

Walking down the bank on Water Way of Low Tide ward to 348 Water Way, they arrive at the Low Bilge tavern. Bloodgrue waits for Lilla to deal with the middle-aged jalmal barkeeper.

Lennie looks at Bloodgrue. Then nodding to Lilla he hands her a coin pouch and they clasp arms.

Lilla walks over to Bloodgrue. "Would you mind unloading the crates for me Bloodgrue? Then Lennie will serve us evening meal before we leave. Being as it is time for evening meal anyway."

Bloodgrue is flabbergasted. Lilla is feeding him a second meal in one day, for him helping her do a simple delivery within North Docks District. Yes, it is in a different ward, but still all in the same day. Some Dyns are just as good, right?

Pulling the cart close to the entry, Bloodgrue carries the six crates into the kitchen for the two clients. When he is finished, Lilla is waiting at a table by the fire-place. On the table are two plates with hot food. There is a cut of beef, tubers and carrots. At Bloodgrue's spot is a large mug of dark ale. He sits down wondering if he will be able to finish the meal. This is the first time in a long time he actually had the luxury of wondering that.

"Thank you Lilla. You didn't have to do this. A simple Dyns payment would have been good."

She touches Bloodgrue's hand gently. "I know, but you pulled the cart and moved the crates. I wanted to thank you Bloodgrue."

Nervously, Bloodgrue's face flushes red and he feels his body heat rise, as her fingers stroke the back of his hand. After a few strokes she pulls away her hand to start eating. Bloodgrue looks into Lilla's face and sees a wistful smile and dreamy eyes, making him even more nervous. He eats his entire meal leaving only bone and gristle on the plate; the mug is empty.

"Well, we should start back." States Bloodgrue hollowly, as they have been in the Low Bilge almost an hour talking and eating.

"We are going to 3497 Elmar Road next, Bloodgrue. Then I will pay you." Instructs Lilla sternly, with a curious smirk.

Bloodgrue again pulls the cart while walking up Water Way. Walking across Osmo Road, and following Elmar Road to 3497, finding it to be a four story apartment building.

Bloodgrue, puzzled, asks. "What are we doing here?"

Lilla chuckles mischievously. "WE are at my place. It is too late for you to go home. You can stay with me for the night Bloodgrue and go at gods-rise."

Bloodgrue frowns, feeling like a trapped animal inside. Outside showing confidence he answers. "I thank you for the offer. Though, the weather is good and I have a client expecting me at my residence, at 4212 Willow Road, at gods-rise. So it is best I head there now, if you could pay me please? I don't want to disappoint my regular client. I am sure you understand Lilla."

Pouting, Lilla offers Bloodgrue. "But I am now a regular client. You will be disappointing me if you leave now."

Bloodgrue nods. "How about we leave with an understanding? You are a regular client as well now. But I have a standing appointment with my other client that I refuse to miss. Okay Lilla? May I collect the one Dyns and be on my way? As it is near mid-night and I need to be at my next client at gods-rise."

Lilla embraces Bloodgrue. Letting him go, she digs out her coin pouch and says. "Show me such loyalty and we will be best friends forever."

With a wink Lila hands Bloodgrue two Dyns, while adding. "For my new favorite dragoman."

Bloodgrue's face turns red and heats up again in the darkness of night. He clasps arms with Lilla, wondering what might have happened. He is sixteen and she is twenty, but he can still guess. He is male and she is a beautiful female asking him to her home.

Bloodgrue walks home fighting with himself for denying Lilla her pleasure, but also knowing it can turn into something he's not ready for.

Mid-early morning, Bloodgrue enters 4212 Willow Road, the debate still raging in him even after all the hours of walking from Lilla's.

Undressing and crawling into his bed with the scratchy wool blanket. '*I bet her bed isn't so uncomfortable*'

Bloodgrue falls asleep quickly.

Summer 2 Raccoon

Bloodgrue's eyes are sore, the light from both gods' shine in his small window. Rubbing his eyes, Bloodgrue ponders yesterday. *'Did I make the right choice?'*

Getting out of bed, Bloodgrue dresses and uses the chamber pot, planning again.

In the kitchen, Bloodgrue remembers what Onar said about his experiences with women.

Onar asks Bloodgrue, as Bloodgrue places a Dyns on the table. "What was your day yesterday?"

Bloodgrue responds. "Normal, I had a client that needed a delivery done. She was impressed enough she said she would be a regular. There is the Dyns from her fees. We are settled now right? I paid the clothes off now?"

Onar thinks a moment then responds. "You paid the clothes off awhile ago Bloodgrue, with the Ottar Marrel run. So we are in the clear again. Sit and eat with me, then we will practice daggers."

Bloodgrue looks at the eggs then shakes his head. "Thank you. I will sit, but I can't eat Master. I look forward to dagger practice."

To be continued …

In the next episode eighteen, *'The Fellow's Mark'*

The Fellow calls on Bloodgrue to help track a mark, they have difficulties and deal with the City Watch before apprehending the mark.

Awesome! You finished an episode of '*Bloodgrue*'.

Let us know what you think of it by going to this this link: www.inupress.ca While you are there, you can join the Inevitable Unicorn Press e-mail subscription list to receive news and updates about work from our authors such as; Rusty Knight, Brian Hill and Aria. When you sign up for the e-mail list, you will receive one free pdf. This free pdf changes with time. In February 2016 the gift was a copy of Rusty Knight's biography of the protagonists, the Black Swans, from his novel, *'Laret'*. Later in 2016, the bonus was an episode from the serial series, *'Lanis'.*

While on the home page of InUPress.ca leave a comment or review telling us what you think of our author's work or your thoughts about the website. We appreciate your time and we will respond to your questions and comments.

Thank you for reading.
Yours,
Rusty Knight of Inevitable Unicorn Press.
www.inupress.ca

Bloodgrue

Fare where?

Rusty Knight

Episode 18, The Fellow's Mark

Bloodgrue
Volume 4: Attractions

Welcome to our serial stories!

If you're not familiar with our serials, think of them as a favorite nighttime program that continues with a new episode each week, only this is in a print format. These are stories that don't necessarily have an end planned for them, or if they do, it's a long way off unlike many television series that we get interested in, only to have them go off air.

Serial stories are a great way to keep you entertained and on edge waiting to see what will happen next, in short enough episodes to enjoy on a lunch break, or before going to bed. Although our stories are designed to be read one episode per week, unlike TV stories, if you just can't wait for the next episode, you can get another one any time.

Be sure to download when you purchase!

It is a good idea to download the episode when you first purchase them. Then, read them at your leisure.

Please feel free to let us know what you think of our serial stories. It's a trend and that may take some getting used to, but we've had positive feedback in the past with them.

Now, it's time to enjoy!

From Rusty Knight & InUPress, Thank you

We would like to acknowledge the following for their work in the production of this series.

Our cover design is by, C S Burgar

All of our editing is by, Donna Shumaker (Aria)

Previously on *Bloodgrue* **Summer 1 Raccoon**,

    Bloodgrue went to Teptun's Square and Market to seek clients. He was approached by Lilla. She hired him to help in delivery of some mugs and plates to Low Tide ward. They had an intimate evening meal at the delivery location of Low Bilge tavern. Then Lilla invited Bloodgrue to stay overnight at her apartment. Bloodgrue hurried home, refusing the offer.

Bloodgrue
By Rusty Knight
Episode 18, 'The Fellow's Mark'

In U Press

Inevitable Unicorn Press

We continue on ….

Summer 14 Raccoon,

The heat has Bloodgrue lounging in the shade of trees, of Onar's courtyard. The gods are being cruel, baking the world and breathing north-west, instead of their usual east. To top it off, they are teasing with scattered cover in the sphere. Bloodgrue is sweating away, drinking water, trying not to overheat.

The courtyard gate opens and in walks a familiar short toymal.

Bloodgrue leaps up and walks over to clasp arms. "How are you, Fellow? It has been awhile. I don't think you heard the news … But Seven Hells … sorry my manners in this heat … Gods-grace and good fate The Fellow, how do you fare?"

The Fellow chuckles, and clasps sweaty arms with Bloodgrue. "I am good. Gods-grace and good fate Bloodgrue, you have news you say? So do I, I have work for you … Interested?"

Bloodgrue laughs heartily. "Under most circumstances I would be jumping all over work. But today I hesitate … But Seven Hells, yes I'll take it since it is you. And I am almost coinless again. What are we doing? Come, have some water and tell me the news."

"Water! Yes, by the gods, yes Bloodgrue, water ... I have a mark for us to hunt down. A runner from government and church, if you think you can handle that."

Bloodgrue pours The Fellow a full mug of cool water and one for himself. They sit in the shade as Bloodgrue peers at The Fellow. "Don't you travel with a skin? I do … it's saved me a lot of time. I will get you one before we leave the house … A runner from Church and King you say. What crime?"

Laughing, The Fellow pulls a poster from his pack. "No, you think I would learn … I'll buy the skin from you Blood. Have you learned toy script yet?" He unfurls the poster. It's in third line toy.

Smiling, Bloodgrue takes the bounty poster. Examining it he replies. "So they offer twenty-five Flairs, saying this Jerred stole two hundred tax Flairs, on his way to the Royal Treasury from the Temple of Ikerus, in Velan District … Nice haul. I might even be tempted, if I was the courier for a church."

He rolls the poster back up and hands it back. "I know toy somewhat, but not jal. Thank you. We'll do it … I think he'll run for the docks to catch a barge, if he's not already gone. Let's try the busy out port. I think our best chance is Anchor's Rest. We can go see the Dock Master; he might have record of a booking on a barge. It'll cost us, but it's a quick start."

"Sounds good. Get your gear and let's walk."

Anchor's Rest was a quick walk of over three and a half hours to the Dock Masters.

Getting the attention of the century-plus Dock Master might take longer. "Excuse me, Gods-grace and good fate Dock Master Trancer, could I have a moment of your time please?"

The old jalmal looks up from his place by the desk. He nods solemnly.

Bloodgrue continues. "A friend of mine is leaving on a barge, but he forgot his Heraldry title from the Church of Ikerus in Velan. His name is Jerred. I was hoping to catch him before the barge leaves. Can you tell me which berth and barge he is on? I'll pay the looking fee."

The old Dock master nods again.

Bloodgrue places a Dyns on the counter and the old dock master looks down his ledger. Stopping on the third page he then gets up and walks to the counter. Picking up the coin he looks it over then says. "He is going out on the freight barge, Fester, They are loading tomorrow, then leaving day after. Good luck boys. Captain Lowern is a nasty piece of work. Doesn't like strangers. Not sure how your friend got booked on board in the first place. Good day to you."

The Fellow places a second Dyns on the counter and says. "Thank you Pampaloo, you helped us a lot; we were afraid we missed our friend. You rest now. Which berth is the Fester at?"

"Oh right, yes … Berth Dock B four. Boys, it's just down on the second dock, second barge on the left hand side."

Bloodgrue offers to clasp arms and says. "Thank you Pampaloo Trancer."

The two men walk along the wide docks of Anchor's Rest, being jostled by the folks along the way. Bloodgrue, frequently checking his nearly empty coin pouch and his short-sword to confirm both are intact.

They approach the second barge on the left at Dock B. The Fellow hails the crew. "Gods-grace and good fate I'm looking for Captain Lowern."

The barge has about 1,500 pounds of cargo on the dock and looks less than half capacity. A mature jalmal moves to the deckhouse and calls inside, he then returns to work. In a short while an elfmal exits the deckhouse and approaches the gangplank. He walks up onto the dock. "You wish to see me?"

The Fellow looks at the elf as if pondering how to follow through on his request, then he comes out with. "Do you have a passenger named Jerred from the Temple of Ikerus on your Barge?"

The elf shakes his head as his only answer.

Bloodgrue places his hand on The Fellow's arm. "Gods-grace and good fate are you Captain Lowern?"

"I am and who would you be?" ask Lowern.

"I am Apprentice Dragoman Bloodgrue. This is my client The Fellow; he is returning some items to Jerred that seem to be forgotten. Is this the barge Fester?"

Captain Lowern nods, answering Bloodgrue. "It is the barge, Fester. May I see these items that you wish to return to this Jerred you seek? Not saying there is a Jerred aboard my barge."

The deckhouse door opens and a jalmal steps out. "Captain, we need to sort out the arrangements for travels on the way to Dendar." The man appears to be about fifty years old and wears Ikerus holy garb. Seeing The Fellow and Bloodgrue he hesitates and Captain Lowern waves him back inside. The man hurries back into the cabin, closing the door.

The Fellow opens his pack while saying. "Okay, enough games. That is the man I am seeking. There is a twenty-five Flair bounty out on him. He is accused of corruption against the Church of Ikerus and the Treasury of the King. Please hand him over."

Lowern walks back onboard the Fester. "You have no rights on the river or aboard my barge. As long as he is aboard the Fester he has sanctuary and I am not handing him over to you."

The Fellow frowns. "Really?"

Lowern nods and responds. "Really."

Bloodgrue smiles and pulls The Fellow away to the center of the dock. "They are a freighter going to Dendar. They need their freight. But if they can't load they won't go. Give me a few minutes. You make sure he doesn't run for it. I'll be back."

"Okay, Blood, but don't be gone long or I will just board that piece of wood and pull him off."

"No, then it won't be legal. Just wait for me, Fellow. Be patient. We are going to use time on our side. Remember, its worth twenty-five Flairs to you. People work years to earn that much. We will do it in less than a few days. Just watch the barge and hope he can't swim."

"Okay, I'll wait."

Bloodgrue heads back towards the shore, looking for a particular kind of person. In less than a hundred metres he finds one. Walking up to her, Bloodgrue address the jalfem. "Excuse me, gods-grace and good fate Master City Watch. Are you a sergeant or private? I haven't learned the stripes yet?"

The woman looks suspiciously at Bloodgrue. "One stripe is private. I am a private. Gods-grace and good fate. I recognize you, your dragoman Bloodgrue. You witnessed for old Blue Hair in Teptun's Square. You did okay for her. What is it you want apprentice?"

Bloodgrue sighs internally, *'this will be easier than I had hoped.'* "I have another one for you private. A friend and I tracked a known criminal to a barge. We have a bounty poster. We spotted and identified the criminal aboard a barge. But the Captain refuses to hand him over to us. I was wondering if you mind confirming it for us. If you confirm and he still refuses, would you blockade the barge until he disembarks or hands over the criminal?"

The private ponders this for a moment then nods. "I will acquire two more privates. What berth and you best be there. We have record of you now and I will personally haunt you if you're pulling one over on me."

Bloodgrue extends his arm, offering a response in return. "I would expect nothing less. What is your name private?"

"I am Private Sanders of Osmo Post."

"Private Sanders, the Barge is the Fester at Berth B four. And I will be there with my friend, The Fellow, a hunter. We brought in another criminal to Sergeant Lamcast several days ago."

"Okay, go back and wait for me Bloodgrue."

"Thank you Private Sanders. I'll be there."

Twenty minutes later Private Sanders arrives with two other privates. They approach Bloodgrue.

Private Sanders addresses him. "So this is the barge?"

"Yes, the Captain is an elf named Lowern. The criminal is a cleric named Jerred who stole two hundred Flairs of tax coins on the way to the Royal Treasury. This toymal is my friend a hunter, The Fellow."

Private Sanders extends her arm. "Gods-grace and good fate The Fellow. You have a bounty poster with you?"

Clasping arms, The Fellow answers with a look of confusion. "Yes I do. But what is happening? Bloodgrue never said anything."

He pulls the poster from his pack and shows it to Sanders, who looks it over then hands it back. She nods to Bloodgrue. "You both saw him onboard?"

"Yes we did."

Sanders turns to The Fellow. "Do you confirm for me that you saw Jerred on board this barge, the Fester?"

The Fellow, suspicious, but knowing the law holds strong powers, answers truthfully. "Yes, yes I do."

Sanders points to one of the other two. "We are going to form a blockade until these two have their bounty in custody, or the Fester leaves port. Go get the blockade crew and inform the Dock Master.

The Fellow, don't worry, we are not taking your bounty. We are blockading the Fester from any further access to the docks until they hand Jerred over to you."

She walks over to the gangplank. "Ahoy there, on the Fester. This is Private Sanders of the City Watch of Mount Oryn; I seek to consult with Captain Lowern."

A crew member goes to the cabin and knocks, then opening the door talks with those inside. Closing the door, he returns to work.

Several minutes later, Captain Lowern exits the cabin and approaches the gangplank. From the barge side he addresses the private. "Gods-grace and good fate how may I be of service Private Sanders?"

Private Sanders wastes no efforts in her address. "You are hereby given notice. The Fester is under blockade until The Fellow and Dragoman Bloodgrue receive custody of the Cleric Jerred. Notice is given. Good day." She turns and walks away without waiting for a reply.

Captain Lowern looks in disbelief as the second Private takes position next to the gangplank and Private Sanders joins Bloodgrue and The Fellow a mere fifteen feet or so from the barge on the dock. Captain Lowern stands looking at them. Then he shakes his head and walks back to his cabin.

Within four hours a crew of eight more City Watch guards arrive to man the blockade of the Fester.

No one is being allowed on or off the Fester for any reason. No cargo is being allowed to be transferred.

Summer 15 Raccoon,

Almost an hour before gods-rise Captain Lowern is standing at the gangplank asking to speak to the one in charge.

Private Sanders rouses Bloodgrue and the Fellow from their sleep in the blankets, by some crates on the dock. The three meet with the Captain.

Private Sanders greets Captain Lowern. "Gods-grace and good fate Captain Lowern, you summon me before gods-rise. Do you wish to speak about something?"

Captain Lowern picks up a large sack with clear heraldry markings of the Church of Ikerus on it. Also near him are three other packs. "I am tired of this. I need to load my freight and get under way today. The longer I wait the more I lose. I searched my passenger's belongings. Your friends will be interested in what I found. It seems they are right. My passenger has an unusually large sum of Royal Flairs with him, in the neighborhood of the sum of the missing taxes. So I would like to turn the bugger over, if you promise to lift the blockade as soon as I do and this incident is stricken from my records."

Private Sanders smiles cheerfully. "I can do that for you Captain Lowern. Did you count the coins then?"

"Yes I did. There are two hundred and eighty-two."

"What happens with them is up to Bloodgrue and the Fellow, as Jerred is their bounty. But as soon as he is in their custody, the blockade will be lifted and if I am satisfied you have done so in good faith, I will lift it from your records." Offers Private Sanders faithfully.

The Fellow looks at Bloodgrue, then shrugging turns to Lowern. "Captain, if you behave in good faith, I offer that you keep twenty of the Flairs from the pack. You bring Jerred to us on the dock. We will take him from you, here. Fair enough?"

All agree and clasp arms. Lowern goes to the cabin and brings a reluctant Jerred to the dock. Sanders witnesses and The Fellow takes custody of Jerred. Counting out twenty Flairs from Jerred's pack, The Fellow pays Captain Lowern.

Private Sanders removes the blockade and the Fester returns to normal activity.

The Fellow addresses Jerred. "You really believe your god would let you steal from him? Or the King would let you steal from him? You would have been tracked to Dendar, if not me someone else then. Believe me; I would go to Dendar for you and twenty-five Flairs. Jerred, you're an idiot. Corruption doesn't really pay in the end. Your god is sending you to the Seven Hells and the King's sending you to the goal for twenty years. You lost, my friend. Let's go."

Jerred resists somewhat, but The Fellow has him carry his three packs, while Bloodgrue carries the coin pouch. Twenty-six pounds is a lot of weight when carrying it for two hours. But eventually they arrive at 3017 Osmo Road, City Watch Post. Entering, they find day-watch Sergeant Lamcast at the desk.

The Fellow steps up to the desk. "Good day. Gods-grace and good fate Sergeant Lamcast, I have another bounty for you." He offers the bounty poster.

Sergeant Lamcast takes the offered poster and standing he says. "Okay, you know the procedure now. Wait here." He leaves, coming back nearly twenty-five minutes later with a similar poster. Lamcast sits, placing a pouch on the desk.

Looking at Bloodgrue, Lamcast nods and then peers at Jerred. Lamcast frowns, obviously connecting him as the bounty mark.

Turning his attention back to The Fellow, Lamcast asks. "The particulars, The Fellow."

The Fellow places the heavy coin pouch on the desk, now with only two hundred Flairs in it. Along with Jerred's three other packs. "I am turning over Cleric Jerred, three packs he was traveling with, and two hundred Flairs of stolen taxes."

Lamcast records this in jal script and then offers it to The Fellow to check over and sign.

They clasp arms, after The Fellow signs the writ.

Sergeant Lamcast gives The Fellow the pouch he had put on his desk.

Bloodgrue and the Fellow leave the watch post.

The Fellow, smiling, offers Bloodgrue six Flairs when they are outside. "My part of the bargain Bloodgrue, ten percent kick back as agreed. Thank you for your help. The kick back includes ten percent from what I kept from his packs. You had a story from last time you were going to tell me?"

Bloodgrue laughs softly. "It doesn't matter. Another time I think. I have to go home now and see if it happens again."

They clasp arms. Bloodgrue walks home to 4212 Willow road. It is evening meal time almost. Bloodgrue walks in the front door of his home. He checks his pouch. Smiling, he enters Onar's living area and hands Onar a Flair. There was a razor cut in the outer skin of his coin pouch but he still had his coins.

We continue on …

In the next episode nineteen, *'Pandora's Job',*

Pandora's House Master Tomar calls on Bloodgrue to go south on a diplomatic mission as Blood of First Rank. On Bloodgrue's journey he has an opportunity to institute a plan regarding the beggar Andolf. Bloodgrue makes some collections from past clients as well.

Awesome! You finished an episode of '*Bloodgrue*'.

Let us know what you think of it by going to this this link: www.inupress.ca While you are there, you can join the Inevitable Unicorn Press e-mail subscription list to receive news and updates about work from our authors such as; Rusty Knight, Brian Hill and Aria. When you sign up for the e-mail list, you will receive one free pdf. This free pdf changes with time. In February 2016 the gift was a copy of Rusty Knight's biography of the protagonists, the Black Swans, from his novel, *'Laret'*. Later in 2016, the bonus was an episode from the serial series, *'Lanis'*.

While on the home page of InUPress.ca leave a comment or review telling us what you think of our author's work or your thoughts about the website. We appreciate your time and we will respond to your questions and comments.

Thank you for reading.
Yours,
Rusty Knight of Inevitable Unicorn Press.
www.inupress.ca

Bloodgrue
Volume 4: Attractions

Welcome to our serial stories!

If you're not familiar with our serials, think of them as a favorite nighttime program that continues with a new episode each week, only this is in a print format. These are stories that don't necessarily have an end planned for them, or if they do, it's a long way off unlike many television series that we get interested in, only to have them go off air.

Serial stories are a great way to keep you entertained and on edge waiting to see what will happen next, in short enough episodes to enjoy on a lunch break, or before going to bed. Although our stories are designed to be read one episode per week, unlike TV stories, if you just can't wait for the next episode, you can get another one any time.

Be sure to download when you purchase!

It is a good idea to download the episode when you first purchase them. Then, read them at your leisure.

Please feel free to let us know what you think of our serial stories. It's a trend and that may take some getting used to, but we've had positive feedback in the past with them.

Now, it's time to enjoy!

From Rusty Knight & InUPress, Thank you

We would like to acknowledge the following for their work in the production of this series.

Our cover design is by, C S Burgar

All of our editing is by, Donna Shumaker (Aria)

Previously on *Bloodgrue **Summer 14 Raccoon**,*

 The Fellow arrived at 4212 Willow Road early in the afternoon seeking Bloodgrue's aid in searching for a mark. The two tracked the mark down to a barge, the Fester docked at B 4, in Anchor's Rest ward. Bloodgrue engaged the City Watch to blockade the barge in an attempted to get an uncooperative elven Captain Lowern, to turn over the mark to The Fellow and Bloodgrue.
 Returning home to 4212 Willow Road, Bloodgrue shared his experience with Onar.

In U Press

Inevitable Unicorn Press

Bloodgrue
By Rusty Knight
Episode nineteen, 'Pandora's Job'

In U Press

Inevitable Unicorn Press

We continue on …

Summer 23 Raccoon,

Bloodgrue is rudely shaken awake in his bed. It is dark except for a small spark of light from a hooded lantern. Opening his eyes, his assailant puts a finger to Bloodgrue's lips for silence.

She shines the meagre light on her own face. It's Luenen. Bloodgrue grins as does Luenen. Getting dressed quickly, Bloodgrue joins Luenen outside on Willow Road.

"What the Seven Hells Luenen? It's at least three hours till gods-rise." Whispers Bloodgrue as he is shivering in the cold.

Luenen giggles then goes serious. "Master Tomar is summoning Bloodgrue of the First Rank for work. He has a job for you. Needs you today, says Master Tomar. Besides, I wanted to see your place while you were sleeping. And you of course."

"Damn Seven Hells. Let me get my things and we will get going." Bloodgrue gears up for traveling and then rejoins Luenen on the street. "So what did you see, girl."

She smirks. "Enough, boy."

They walk together through a very cold partially covered day, to Pandora House.

Arriving at 1214 Pickers Street, Luenen gestures to the door. "Do you remember?"

Laughing, Bloodgrue walks up to the door and knocks. Upon hearing, "What Temple?" Bloodgrue answers. "Joyn of Lorn for Pandora."

The door quickly swings open and three guards with their clubs ready stand inside, waving the two travelers in.

Stepping in, Luenen leads Bloodgrue through the late day throng to the back and through the door into the stairwell. They go up the stairs to the fourth floor. Arriving on the fourth floor they come to the lieutenant reception area.

Annalee stands up quickly from her desk, smiling. She embraces Bloodgrue before he can object. He returns the embrace; they engage in conversation. "So the new job's working out for you Annalee?"

Annalee, still smiling, replies energetically. "It's an opportunity I never had with my old guild. I am a Second Lieutenant of training, and a guide of juniors and new recruits. Thank you so much apprentice. I owe you more than the five percent of my income that we agreed upon. The apartment you found me is beautiful. Better than my old place and cheaper. Though it is a bit of a walk from here, it is a little over an hour. I wouldn't trade it … Here, my dues I owe you, the full two Flairs, seven Dyns and one duster to date, as agreed to."

She digs in a drawer of her desk and retrieves a coin pouch, handing it to Bloodgrue with a genuinely happy smile.

Bloodgrue takes the pouch. He empties its contents into his special pouch, which he recently had repaired. Bloodgrue gives back the coin pouch to Annalee. "Thank you Annalee. Keep it from now on and pay on the first of each season. Send it courier to 4212 Willow Road, if I don't pick it up, okay?"

Annalee puts the pouch back in the drawer and clasps arms with Bloodgrue. "Agreed, pay on the first of the season, couriered to 4212 Willow Road."

Luenen knocks on a sturdy maple wood door. A masculine voice calls forth. "Enter."

Opening the door, Luenen gestures for Bloodgrue to follow.

They enter Tomar's den; it is a boldly dark room of wood and plaster. Lit by three lanterns, there are no windows. A sturdy oak desk and three guest chairs and one padded desk chair, and a small table adorn the room. Two book shelves line the east and west walls. A carpet covers the entire floor. A sturdy Walnut chest, with steel fastenings and binding, stands near the oak desk. It has a strong keyed lock holding it shut. Four paintings adorn two of the walls, two on each wall.

Tomar remains seated, pointing to the guest chairs he utters indifferently. "Sit."

Bloodgrue and Luenen take seats apart from each other.

Tomar, not pretending to be fooled by the lack of affection, continues. "Bloodgrue, I am sending you on a diplomatic mission. You are going to recruit for me, a master gambler and artisan, if you can. I have sent several others and they failed. I want you to try for me. In return you can take Luenen with you to do what we talked about earlier. I have a diplomatic pouch ready. The two of you can stay here tonight and leave in the morning. Luenen, watch over him to the point we agreed to."

Bloodgrue smirks evilly. "Thank you Master Tomar. I will do what I can. What address am I going to?"

Tomar looks at a note on his desk then responds. "2064 Pedmonton Avenue. Do you know it?"

Bloodgrue ponders this for a moment then replies questioningly. "I believe it is in Archoman ward, about thirty kilometres from here. It will be a few days before I can return with an answer Master Tomar. What can I offer this recruit?"

Tomar smiles, further encouraged. "I like you still. You go right to the meat. Okay, we may supply a local apartment or house, up to seven Dyns a day, things in ranges like that Bloodgrue. But I prefer you stay at around five Dyns a day or less and don't get too crazy with housing. If you know of housing within three hours of here for less than a Dyns a day, you can offer it to her. This is a renowned gambler, named Pambala, a jalfem who can teach my recruits things to watch for. So I really would like this pampamoo in my stable. If you can do it, there is a bonus for you. If not, don't worry, I won't remove your testicles this time. You will get your standard Dragoman fee, to keep your master happy."

Bloodgrue smiles enigmatically. He offers his arm to clasp and Tomar correspondingly accepts, clasping arms with Bloodgrue.

"Okay, you are dismissed. Luenen, ask Annalee for Diplomatic pouch three and you take that, Bloodgrue."

The pair rise and exit.

In the reception area, Luenen addresses Annalee. "Tomar approves diplomatic pouch three to be released to Bloodgrue."

Annalee goes to a large chest and retrieves a small pack. Smirking, she hands it to Bloodgrue. "Good luck apprentice. I hear this one is a tough nut to crack."

Bloodgrue clasps arms with Annalee and smiling says. "We will see what happens, won't we."

Luenen and Bloodgrue retire to the third floor common room for the remainder of the evening.

Summer 24 Raccoon,

Bloodgrue spots Andolf before being spotted. It is almost two hours into the afternoon already. Bloodgrue points him out to Luenen. "That's him. Is he one of yours?"

Luenen nods. "Yes, but a sour one. We have fined him a time or two. He's on report and probation. Let's deal with this properly like Tomar said. I have the paper work. It will be dealt with Blood, then I will return to Pandora House like we agreed."

Bloodgrue hugs Luenen then straightening up and going business like, the two walk toward Andolf.

"Gods-grace and good fate Andolf we have business to tend to, the three of us." calls forth, a business commanding Bloodgrue.

Andolf reaches for his club and utters angrily. "After you pay your tithe of one Dyns, boyo."

Luenen steps forward and taking a folded parchment from her belt pouch, she says. "You will not harass or collect from Bloodgrue in the future for any purposes, by order of Master Tomar and Captain Pandora, herself. Breach of this will be banishment from Pandora territory at best, Andolf. Understood? This is the order signed and sealed by both authorities and witnessed by two lieutenants. I witnessed it delivered to you as of today, Summer 24 Raccoon. Know it is reported; you just tried to collect a one Dyns fee from Bloodgrue. Do you still wish to try to collect that?"

Andolf takes the parchment. He carefully reads the writ, then looking at the two with new respect he turns to Bloodgrue. "My apologies Master, I was unaware of your title and connections. We no longer have an arrangement of collections. You may pass freely and if I may ever be of service, please ask, Master Bloodgrue. Again … my apologies, Master Bloodgrue."

Luenen, waiting, looks at Bloodgrue.

Bloodgrue nods, satisfied. "Apology accepted, Master Andolf, and to show respect and no hard feelings, please accept my freely giving of one Dyns." Bloodgrue places a Dyns into Andolf's bowl. The man beams a wide smile as Bloodgrue offers to clasp arms. The three clasp arms in acknowledgement of the truce.

Luenen hugs Bloodgrue, who returns the embrace. "I must return to Pandora House now to report to Tomar. Good luck Blood … I didn't say it earlier, but I like your place … Can I visit, besides at the middle of the night?"

Bloodgrue, shocked anyone would want to visit him at Onar's, but is elated Luenen wants to, nods as he replies. "Yes, of course silly. I should say so."

Luenen skips off, obviously happy.

Bloodgrue nods to Andolf, who smiles and nods back in return.

Bloodgrue returns to his journey.

Summer 25 Raccoon,

2064 Pedmonton Avenue is an unassuming stone and wood structure, two stories tall with a thatched roof. Bloodgrue knocks on the door, not certain on what greeting to expect.

A jalfem, who looks like she is a century old, answers the door, greeting Bloodgrue with. "Yah, what do you want?" in perfect jal.

Bloodgrue, not certain he is going to be able to match language ability with her, does his best jal. "Gods-grace and good fate pampamoo Pambala, I seek council with you if you allow?"

The old crone seems to soften slightly. "You know my name. I don't recognize you. Did someone send you? I have no debts, so you can't be from a collector. What is it you seek? What's your name boy?"

Bloodgrue, still not sure which side of the barge this is going to go, opens up to Pambala. "Master Pambala, I am Apprentice Dragoman Bloodgrue, also, Bloodgrue of First Rank for Pandora. I come to discuss a matter with you as Bloodgrue of First Rank for Pandora, not as apprentice dragoman. I wish to be honest with you right from the start."

Pambala looks at Bloodgrue blankly for a few moments then she waves Bloodgrue in. "You can talk; doesn't mean I'll answer you Bloodgrue. I give you points for being forth right with me."

Inside himself, Bloodgrue sighs, feeling the barge has balanced.

Going into Pambala's house, it is neat and tidy, filled with mementos and memorabilia from times and events she has passed through.

Bloodgrue wants to know her a little, so he observes her house as they walk to the common room. There Pambala serves Bloodgrue tea as they settle down to talk. The tea is lukewarm, as she made it a while ago for herself. Bloodgrue, happy it's not just water, or ale, courteously drinks politely. "Master Pambala, I come to you only knowing what Master Tomar told me. I wish to know the truth of matters before I speak on Tomar's behalf. May I ask you some questions?"

Pambala, swayed even closer to liking Bloodgrue, nods a simple affirmative but doesn't speak.

Bloodgrue, taking the meaning, begins. "Please tell me your profession. I don't care what the Royal treasurer lists as your profession, what is it you actually made your living at?"

Pambala laughs heartily. "Lad, I am a gambler with a reputation as one of the most feared. I made a fortune gaming. And still do. I paid for my house and raised my family gaming. I retired gaming and pay my taxes gaming. The treasurer believes I am a scribe. Go on."

Bloodgrue continues. "Then am I correct; you own your house Fee Simple?"

She nods in answer.

"Would, if we could arrange it, you consider keeping your home but work elsewhere and stay for short times close to work?"

Pambala looks at Bloodgrue quizzically. "This sounds like the job offer coming up again. It would depend on a lot of things, Bloodgrue."

Bloodgrue nods thoughtfully then decides he is ready to open negotiations with Pambala. "Well Master, it is a job negotiation I am here for. I was sent to offer you a second lieutenant job as instructor and guide to juniors. It has benefits and wages if you're interested in it."

Pambala looks at Bloodgrue humorously, replying animatedly. "They have made offers and threats before. I refused. What is different this time?"

Bloodgrue smiles openly, pointing to his diplomatic pouch. "In that pouch I brought coins with me. I am prepared to leave ten Flairs with you today."

Pambala shakes her head. "Those coins don't interest me. I can make that much gaming in one session."

Bloodgrue bows politely. "Then how about I leave you twenty Flairs today?"

Pambala hesitates this time and looks at the pouch. "Twenty Flairs still doesn't do it. But you're getting my attention now."

Bloodgrue, trying to determine if perhaps housing is the issue; offers. "Then, how about I just leave the twenty Flairs with you, while you think about this. But I know of a nice two room second floor apartment, forty minutes walk from work, that you might like and the employer will pay the rent on."

Pambala leans forward looking into Bloodgrue's face. Bloodgrue feels he is onto something here. Pambala answers softly. "I won't do stairs."

Bloodgrue nods, understanding, but not mentioning the stairs at Pandora House, he offers. "Okay, I know of a one story three room house, sixty minutes from the employer, they will pay the rent on it."

She smiles. "I like that, but I'm not convinced. What are the wages?"

Bloodgrue eeks out a small yes inside, one-point won. "Okay, so you accept a house. The wages are a flat rate, five Dyns per day worked."

Pambala balks and sits backs. Bloodgrue, noticing the change in posture, tries to recover the talks. "How about, we get you a better house? Within ten minutes of Teptun's Square and Market with a maid?"

Pambala immediately shifts again, sitting forward, again eyeing Bloodgrue. "Leave your pack and the open contract with me. I will think about it with those conditions attached."

Bloodgrue, seeing interest peeked, not wanting to push and break the interest, answers. "Okay then, I will take that news to Master Tomar. Master Pambala, when you are ready with your answer, send a messenger to my residence at 4212 Willow Road and I will inform the employer. Fair enough?"

Pambala rises and offers her arm to clasp. "Fair by me, thank you Bloodgrue."

Bloodgrue clasps arms with Pambala.

Even though it is close to gods-set Bloodgrue departs so as not to upset the balance.

Getting a kilometre away, Bloodgrue finds a woodshed, at nearly god-set, to sleep the night in.

Summer 27 Raccoon,

Bloodgrue had force marched back to Pandora House, walking more than twelve hours' yesterday. Bloodgrue arrived back at Pandora House just before evening meal today. The extreme heat yesterday had Bloodgrue stop and fill his skin four times. Compared to today's cold where he barely drank any water, filling his skin only once. Arriving at 1214 Pickers Street, he ate the last of his hard tack an hour ago. He has half a skin of water left. Knocking on the door, Bloodgrue follows protocol.

Inside, he is greeted by Luenen at the fourth floor reception area.

"How did it go?" She asks eagerly.

Bloodgrue, tired to near exhaustion and wishing to conserve further energy, shrugs and knocks on Tomar's door, waving Luenen to join him.

Tomar's voice rings out. "Enter."

The two friends enter the den.

Bloodgrue proceeds. "We don't have an answers but it looks good. I offered her a house near Teptun's Square with a maid and five Dyns per day. She seemed very interested, but asked for time to think about it. She will send me her answer when she is ready. I left the twenty Flairs and your contract with her."

Tomar beams happily. "That's the best response we managed so far. Thank you. Luenen, tell Annalee to pay Bloodgrue three Dyns Dragoman fee and one Dyns Diplomat fee. Now you two get out."

They exit Tomar's office, leaving a happy House Master.

In reception, Annalee pays Bloodgrue the four Dyns.

Bloodgrue spends the night in the bunk room again, before going home to Onar.

Summer 33 Raccoon,

just after gods-rise as Onar is eating the morning meal prepared by Bloodgrue, a messenger arrives for Bloodgrue. The young toyfem addresses Bloodgrue. "Master Pambala regrets to inform you that though your offer entices her dearly, her advanced age prevents Master Pambala from accepting the contract and any future offers will likely likewise be rejected. Thank you for the twenty Flairs and the nice time over tea, Master Bloodgrue. But the offer is declined. As per Master Pambala."

Bloodgrue tips the messenger two dusters as he curses under his breath, 'Seven Hells, now I have to inform Tomar and Luenen."

Louder, so Master Onar can hear, Bloodgrue says. "I have to forego lessons today, Master Onar. I have to give a client a message as soon as I can reach them. Please excuse me; I will finish up with morning chores then leave."

Onar simply acknowledges with a wave of his hand and continues to eat; as long as he's getting wealthier from Bloodgrue's activities he's happy. And lately Bloodgrue's contributions have picked up considerably.

To be continued …

In the next episode twenty, *'Anchor's Rest Clients'*

Traveling back to Teptun Square and Market Bloodgrue is hired and runs a string of jobs. Being questionable on some.

Awesome! You finished an episode of '*Bloodgrue*'.

Let us know what you think of it by going to this this link: www.inupress.ca While you are there, you can join the Inevitable Unicorn Press e-mail subscription list to receive news and updates about work from our authors such as; Rusty Knight, Brian Hill and Aria. When you sign up for the e-mail list, you will receive one free pdf. This free pdf changes with time. In February 2016 the gift was a copy of Rusty Knight's biography of the protagonists, the Black Swans, from his novel, *'Laret'*. Later in 2016, the bonus was an episode from the serial series, *'Lanis'*.

While on the home page of InUPress.ca leave a comment or review telling us what you think of our author's work or your thoughts about the website. We appreciate your time and we will respond to your questions and comments.

Thank you for reading.
Yours,
Rusty Knight of Inevitable Unicorn Press.
www.inupress.ca

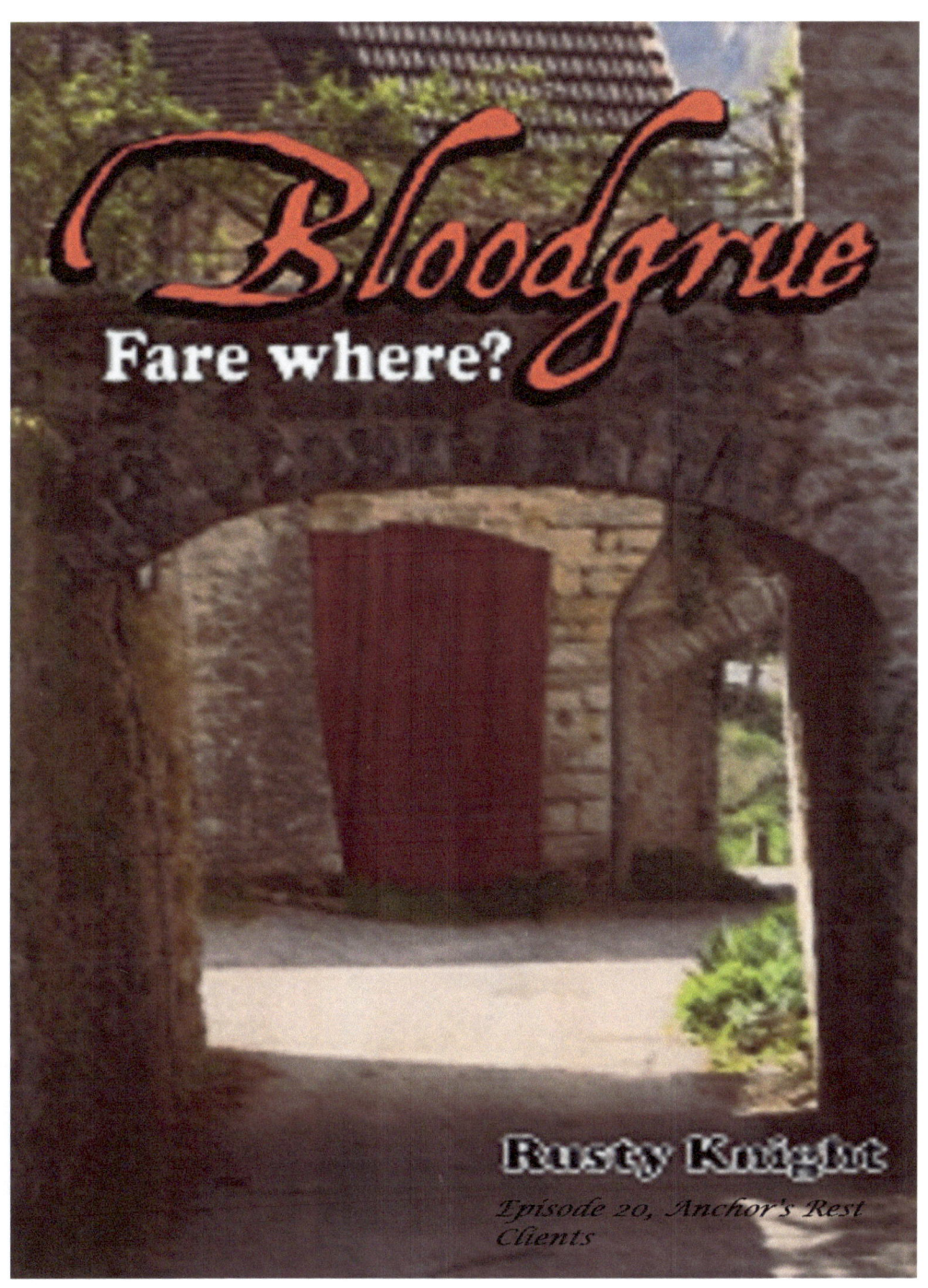

Bloodgrue

Fare where?

Rusty Knight

Episode 20, Anchor's Rest
Clients

Bloodgrue
Volume 4: Attractions

Welcome to our serial stories!

If you're not familiar with our serials, think of them as a favorite nighttime program that continues with a new episode each week, only this is in a print format. These are stories that don't necessarily have an end planned for them, or if they do, it's a long way off unlike many television series that we get interested in, only to have them go off air.

Serial stories are a great way to keep you entertained and on edge waiting to see what will happen next, in short enough episodes to enjoy on a lunch break, or before going to bed. Although our stories are designed to be read one episode per week, unlike TV stories, if you just can't wait for the next episode, you can get another one any time.

Be sure to download when you purchase!

It is a good idea to download the episode when you first purchase them. Then, read them at your leisure.

Please feel free to let us know what you think of our serial stories. It's a trend and that may take some getting used to, but we've had positive feedback in the past with them.

Now, it's time to enjoy!

From Rusty Knight & InUPress, Thank you

We would like to acknowledge the following for their work in the production of this series.

Our cover design is by, C S Burgar
All of our editing is by, Donna Shumaker (Aria)

Bloodgrue
Volume 4: Attractions

Previously on *Bloodgrue* **Summer 23 Raccoon**,

Pandora's House Master Tomar hired Bloodgrue to go south as a diplomat, to recruit an old pampamoo gambler as a trainer for his juniors and recruits. On Bloodgrue's journey he instituted a plan for dealing with Andolf by taking Luenen with Bloodgrue. Annalee paid Bloodgrue for finding her the rescue job.

Bloodgrue
By Rusty Knight
Episode twenty, 'Anchor's Rest Clients'

In U Press

Inevitable Unicorn Press

We continue on…

Summer 43 Raccoon,

Bloodgrue is not feeling particularly like following through with lessons; he decides working feels better. Walking out of 4212 Willow Road before gods-rise, into early heat, Bloodgrue wonders if the broken cover will clear or solidify overhead. The average breathes of the gods are oddly north-east, which might be a bad omen for today, or might be why Bloodgrue is restless. None-the-less Bloodgrue is headed to Teptun's Square and Market to look for clients.

Arriving in Teptun's before noon, Bloodgrue beats around the open shops looking for clients. At stall 18, Master Herbalist Zandel waves Bloodgrue over. "Gods-grace and good fate apprentice. I need your service. Are you available?" enquires the old jalmal in his trade accented jal.

Bloodgrue bows politely and responds in clear jal. "Gods-grace and good fate Master Zandel, I am available. How may I be of service?"

Frowning, Zandel quips quickly. "I have a delivery I must send my apprentice with. I would like you to escort him. We will pay your Dragoman's fee."

Bloodgrue nods. "Consider it done Master. What address?"

Master Zandel motions to a teenage jalmal. "Get the pack, Morson, you are going with Bloodgrue."

Turning to Bloodgrue, Zandel instructs him. "The address is the Tessen residence at 242 Yarrow Street in Anchor's Rest ward. Standard fee, right?"

Bloodgrue nods. "Yes Master. One Dyns for the service."

Morson arrives quickly with a carrier's pouch. Bloodgrue notes the boy looks healthy, but may not have much endurance, from his appearance. "We will be on our way then. It is about five or six kilometres to this residence."

They walk for a little over three hours and arrive at 242 Yarrow Street. Bloodgrue knocks on the door. A jalmal teen answers the door. Croaking hoarsely, he answers Bloodgrue in broken jal. "Yes … what do you want?"

Bloodgrue backs up, knowing a sick person when meeting one. "Is this the Tessen residence?"

The teen replies sadly. "Yes, it is."

Bloodgrue turns to Morson, who hasn't spoken a word since leaving Stall 18 in Teptun's. "You owe me a Dyns. This is your client."

Morson pays Bloodgrue a Dyns silently, then approaches the boy at the door, offering him the parcel. The sick teen accepts the parcel, confused. So Bloodgrue approaches. "It is from Herbalist Zandel, in Teptun's Square and Market."

The boy nods. "Oh … this must be the herbs ordered by Healer Tuscany for my throat. Thank you."

Bloodgrue take Morson away from the house. "Can you find your way back?"

Morson smiles and nods eagerly. Bloodgrue clasps arms with him and they part ways.

Thinking for a moment, Bloodgrue decides to seek a client in the Duck Tavern.

Walking over to 234 Wendel Avenue, Bloodgrue enters. Spotting the barkeeper Gena, he waves to her.

Gena engages Bloodgrue cheerfully in jal. "Gods-grace and good fate apprentice, what do you bring me?"

Bloodgrue beams his now renowned grin. "Good fate is what I bring. Sorry, no customers. I will buy a dark ale, though and observe your clients, for clients for myself. You haven't heard anyone looking for services I could render?"

Gena laughs heartily then responds. "No, no clients for you. One dark ale, for two dusters Bloodgrue. Have a seat at the bar. If anyone is looking for help I'll send them to you."

Gena taps an ale for Bloodgrue and he pays her.

Sitting watching and listening to people come and go, Bloodgrue spends about forty minutes, when a leather armour wearing jalmal, his long-sword showing some use, sits next to Bloodgrue. The man looks at Bloodgrue and in rough jal he says. "Friend, might I buy you an ale?"

Bloodgrue ponder this then nods, yes. It is almost evening meal time. He should consider going home. But one more ale, that could become a client, will be fine.

The man waves over Gena and orders two ales. He offers his arm to Bloodgrue to clasp. "My name's Everleaf; I am a Ranger from north of the river. I was in town to sell my dragon hide. Got a good price and I'm headed back north now. Want to hear about my story?"

'Ranger? Dragon hide? Could be interesting right?' "Sure Everleaf. I'm Apprentice Dragoman Bloodgrue, well met." Bloodgrue clasps arms with Everleaf.

Gena leaves the two be, as Everleaf begins his tale. "I was riding my steed, the black mare, Night-tide, out of the hills north of Archeron Desert, onto the flats of the desert when I spotted a red dragon. I cautiously rode out to meet the dragon. Seeing the dragon was a threat, I engaged in mortal combat striking true. I wounded the beast. It flew off in fear of me. I rode it down, upon Night-tide until I was again upon it when the beast landed. I attacked it again, as it breathed its fiery breath of death, killing Night-tide in a stream of flames. I managed to survive the flames and strike the beast with my sword, again wounding it. It flew off, yet again in fear of me. I ran it down, following until it landed again. I attacked the dragon until I slew it. Once it was dead, I ate of its heart and brain and gained its true name. It was Spot-fire. I skinned it of its hide and carried it out of the desert, south to the river and here to the Mage's University. They paid me five thousand Flairs for the hide of the beast."

What Everleaf fails to mention, is he snuck up on the sleeping juvenile dragon, who was basking in the gods-light of the open. He drove his sword into a startled dragon whose reflex was to fly off. Being as his wing was wounded he could only fly a few hundred metres. Everleaf was able to watch him the whole way and rode quickly to him. And when he got close he jumped behind his horse when the dragon breathed. Running at the ten-foot-long, ten-year-old dragon he drove his sword into its other wing. It tried to fly off, but only got a few dozen metres. Everleaf followed and as he tripped on a rock, his sword drove into the heart of the dragon, killing it. He ate the heart and brain, because when the dragon toasted his horse, his supplies were toasted and he was hungry and short of supplies. The dragon's true name is actually, Spot. An actual adult dragon hide is worth over 50,000 Flairs to the mages.

Bloodgrue appears suitably impressed, not sure dragons actually exist and that the man isn't sniffing too much smoke or drinking too much hard liquor. "Sounds impressive Master Everleaf. Safe travels to you on your journeys in the future. May you succeed always in you endeavours."

Bloodgrue is rescued from further tales of grandeur, by a mature jalfem who is introduced by Gena. Gena offers. "Dragoman Bloodgrue, this is Master Lezbet, she needs a Dragoman's service. I will leave you two be."

Bloodgrue stands and greets Lezbet. "Gods-grace and good fate Master Lezbet how may I be of service?

Lezbet bows slightly. "I have been contracted to a job in Low Docks ward. I was hoping to arrive today. Would you mind escorting me to my new employer, Dragoman Bloodgrue?"

Bloodgrue shows his grin and then answers. "Master Lezbet I would be honored. The fee is three dusters, up front. Then we can be on our way. Tell me our destination."

Lezbet digs into the meagre contents of her coin pouch. "I am going to the warehouse at 7 River Way Avenue. Can you find it for me?"

Bloodgrue nods knowingly. "Yes, it is easy enough, we will be there shortly. Follow me." He says as he puts away his new coins.

Bloodgrue escorts Lezbet to 7 River Way Avenue in Low Tide ward. Then he bids her a good day.

Looking up at the gods he determines less than two hours of gods-light remains. Yet it is about six hours' home and there is small point to gathering a client now. So Bloodgrue walks over to the Drop Bucket on 137 Water Way Street.

Entering he finds Innkeeper Henney Mae and books a room for the night for a Dyns.

Leaving the Drop Bucket, well before gods-rise, Bloodgrue arrives at 4212 Willow Road at almost two in the afternoon. He enters the residence and business of Master Onar and himself, looking for Onar.

Going into Onar's living area, Bloodgrue finds Onar looking at a picture with strange lines and markings.

"Master Onar, I have more coin for you and a strange tale. A fellow, calling himself a Ranger, told me a story of his slaying of a dragon and eating its heart and brain. Giving him its true name and how he carried its hide out, earning a payment of five thousand Flairs from the Mages."

Onar looks at Bloodgrue blandly.

Smirking suddenly, he asks. "Do you believe him?"

Bloodgrue responds. "I don't know. Are there really Dragons? Would anyone pay anyone five thousand Flairs for anything?"

Onar bursts out laughing heartily. Calming down, he points to his parchment. "Did he tell you where he slew the dragon?"

"Yes, the Archeron Desert, south of the hills."

Onar looks at the drawing. Then points to a yellow patch and says. "This is a map, Bloodgrue, and this here is the Archeron Desert, just north of the river about seventy kilometres. But the hills are sixty kilometres across the desert, from the river. So to get to the river, your ranger needed to carry a dragon hide across sixty kilometres of the nastiest desert in our realm. Then seventy kilometres of unforgiving forest lands. Then cross the four kilometres of the river. He would then have to get to and into the Mage's University. No small feat. Dragons do exist Bloodgrue. There used to be hundreds of them. But last I heard there hasn't been one reported, for over two hundred years that anyone can get close to. Three ancients exist that are reported. Now dragon's hide weighs anywhere from five to ten pounds per square foot depending on variety and age. Did he say how old it was, or what type or how big?"

Bloodgrue ponders the question for a bit then shaking his head he answers. "I think all I recall is red dragon."

Onar ponders this, and then answers. "None of the ancients are reds. And records I recall, mention red hides weight on average seven pounds a square foot. So if he had an adult at twenty feet long, for a small one say. For argument's sake four hundred square feet of hide. That would be twenty-eight hundred pounds of dragon hide. He didn't carry it out. But if he did, the last one I recall was sold for sixty-seven thousand Flairs for a red adult. How much did you say he got for his hide?"

Bloodgrue blurts out, baffled by the numbers and Onar's knowledge. "Five thousand."

"So he sold them a small chunk, or a baby. At the largest, it was a juvenile, Bloodgrue, if he sold them a hide for five thousand. Likely, it was a dragon hide. Likelihood, if he carried it across the Archeron and through the wood to the mages, it was a red, but not an adult or mature. He was telling you a tale for sure. What the truth is you won't know, apprentice. Likely he found or killed a dragon and sold part of the hide to the mage's university at a fraction of the true price. He likely doesn't know the true name of the dragon. If he ate the brain and heart and got the dragon power reputed to be gained, he wouldn't speak of it lightly. Use caution, true, but don't dismiss out right folks' tales to you Bloodgrue."

Bloodgrue starts his chores as he thinks about what Onar told him. He also ponders the picture on Onar's desk.

To be continued …

In the next episode twenty-one, *'Blue Hair's Request'*,

Blue Hair grants Bloodgrue work that takes the dragoman on a long trek.

Awesome! You finished an episode of '*Bloodgrue*'.

Let us know what you think of it by going to this this link: www.inupress.ca While you are there, you can join the Inevitable Unicorn Press e-mail subscription list to receive news and updates about work from our authors such as; Rusty Knight, Brian Hill and Aria. When you sign up for the e-mail list, you will receive one free pdf. This free pdf changes with time. In February 2016 the gift was a copy of Rusty Knight's biography of the protagonists, the Black Swans, from his novel, *'Laret'*. Later in 2016, the bonus was an episode from the serial series, *'Lanis'*.

While on the home page of InUPress.ca leave a comment or review telling us what you think of our author's work or your thoughts about the website. We appreciate your time and we will respond to your questions and comments.

Thank you for reading.
Yours,
Rusty Knight of Inevitable Unicorn Press.
www.inupress.ca

Bloodgrue

Fare where?

Rusty Knight

Episode 21, Blue Hair's Request

Bloodgrue
Volume 4: Attractions

Welcome to our serial stories!

If you're not familiar with our serials, think of them as a favorite nighttime program that continues with a new episode each week, only this is in a print format. These are stories that don't necessarily have an end planned for them, or if they do, it's a long way off unlike many television series that we get interested in, only to have them go off air.

Serial stories are a great way to keep you entertained and on edge waiting to see what will happen next, in short enough episodes to enjoy on a lunch break, or before going to bed. Although our stories are designed to be read one episode per week, unlike TV stories, if you just can't wait for the next episode, you can get another one any time.

Be sure to download when you purchase!

It is a good idea to download the episode when you first purchase them. Then, read them at your leisure.

Please feel free to let us know what you think of our serial stories. It's a trend and that may take some getting used to, but we've had positive feedback in the past with them.

Now, it's time to enjoy!

From Rusty Knight & InUPress, Thank you

We would like to acknowledge the following for their work in the production of this series.

Our cover design is by, C S Burgar

All of our editing is by, Donna Shumaker (Aria)

Bloodgrue
Volume 4: Attractions

Previously on *Bloodgrue* **Summer 43 Raccoon**,

    Traveling into Teptun's Square & Market, Bloodgrue was hired by Master Herbalist Zandel to escort his apprentice to Anchor's Rest ward and make a delivery to their client. Having done so, the apprentice paid Bloodgrue and departed.

    Bloodgrue went to the Duck tavern and was regaled by the Ranger Everleaf with his exploits north of the river. After listening to the tale of dragon slaying, Bloodgrue was rewarded by being petitioned by an actual client needing to go to Low Tide ward at 7 River Way Avenue.

In U Press

Inevitable Unicorn Press

Bloodgrue
By Rusty Knight
Episode twenty-one, 'Blue Hair's Request'

We continue on ...

Summer 60 Raccoon,

Bloodgrue finishes his chores and skips lessons to go to Teptun Square & Market to look for work again. The gods are at it again, they are breathing south and have placed broken cover in the sphere. This odd behaviour worked last time for Bloodgrue; let's see if it works again.

Walking the approximately three and a half hours to the Square & Market, Bloodgrue peers out over the various stalls and shops from his position in the eastern entry. The square is crowded, as it is noon.

Bloodgrue wades out into the masses looking for clients. Unthinking, he gravitates towards the central fountain and finds himself at Blue Hair's stall 74. Blue Hair waves Bloodgrue over excitedly.

"Apprentice are you just wandering around? Would you like a job?" asks Bloodgrue's matronly mentor.

Bloodgrue grins his renowned smile. "Of course I seek work, Blue Hair. Gods-grace and good fate my friend."

Blue Hair claps her hands together, excited. "Yes, gods-grace and good fate, apprentice dragoman. This here is freight master Raster. She needs to go south and have an escort back over to Lance's Mercenary Ward. It will be a challenge though, even for you." Blue Hair gestures towards a forty-year-old appearing jalfem standing near at hand with three horses. She has two riding horses and a pack horse.

Bloodgrue suddenly is nervous and has a question. "Gods-grace and good fate Master Raster. But why do you have horses? Is there someone else with you?"

Raster frowns and asks disheartened. "You can't ride, can you? The second horse is for my dragoman. We are riding."

Blue Hair places her hand on Bloodgrue's shoulder. "You'll learn quickly. It's not that bad ... I rode for years while in service to the King. Really Blood, my boy ... You will be fine. Just take it easy. Let the horse do the work."

Bloodgrue frowns. Never having been on a horse, he answers Raster. "No, I have never ridden a horse ... Not even a toy horse."

Bloodgrue looks at Blue Hair, sarcastically remarking. "You owe me a favour for this, if I make it."

Walking over to the horses, Bloodgrue says to Raster nervously. "Which one do I ride?"

Raster smiles harmlessly. "You get the six-year-old mare. Her name is Buttercup ... She is gentle and easy to work with. Let her lead ... I'll help you. Let me show you how to mount, and sit ... Get over on her left side."

Bloodgrue walks to Buttercup's left side and begins to stroke her mane. He is wondering who is more nervous, him or her.

Raster gives Bloodgrue three carrots and says. "Stash two in your pouch. Offer her one now. When you're both ready, take a handful of her mane with the same hand you're holding her rein. Grab the saddle with the other hand, as you have your left foot in the stirrup. Raise yourself and swing your right leg over and insert your right foot in the stirrup on the other side. Relax your ass into the saddle, but keep some weight evenly distributed on the stirrups slightly. Not much to it. Stroke her neck and talk with her. Then let go of her mane. And you can relax … You should be ready. It will be awkward at first, but settle in."

Bloodgrue awkwardly does as instructed and in a couple attempts is onboard Buttercup, shy one carrot and nervous as all seven hells.

"Okay, where are we going Master Raster? … And Blue Hair, I am going to collect." Bloodgrue states strongly.

Raster smiles, and then states. "I am looking for 427 Arcmor Avenue, Hacarn Forge. Can you find it?"

Bloodgrue searches the archives of his mental maps, then nods. "Yes. It is south about forty-five kilometres. It's an older long established forge in the Warrior ward. It will take a couple days to get to. Let's go."

Bloodgrue tenderly leads south, down to the Fifth Street South Road exit. They make good time and as they pass Andolf, Bloodgrue acknowledges the beggar politely. Andolf returns the acknowledgement friendlily.

Summer 62 Raccoon,

The day dragged on with the heat magnifying Bloodgrue's discomfort. Having been riding Buttercup for more than two days his ass and thighs ache. Bloodgrue is sure he has blisters he doesn't want to know about.

Bloodgrue brings Buttercup to a stop in front of the large forge at 427 Arcmor Avenue. Reading the sign; that is in both jal, and in toy third line script, it reads, Hacarn Forge. Bloodgrue gingerly dismounts from the horse and feeds it his last carrot.

"This is your stop. Let's get what you came for." Bloodgrue takes the reins of Raster's two horses and waits.

Raster takes two sacks in to the building with her. Spending nearly an hour in the forge, she then comes out with two large wrapped, four-foot-long bundles.

Bloodgrue peers at them. "So what do you have?"

Raster settles the bundles on the pack horse as she explains. "These are two bundles of six long-swords each. Each sword is worth forty-five Flairs. We need to be cautious returning to Lance's Mercenary Docks Ward."

Bloodgrue nods slowly. Then he asks enquiringly. "Which barracks are we going to?"

Raster finishes tying the last bundle onto the pack horse and informs Bloodgrue. "We are going to the Blue Doves, on Fourth Street."

Bloodgrue checks to confirm his dagger is in its place in his waist band and that his short-sword is ready if needed.

The two mount up again and head east, along Arcmor Avenue. Over the next days they travel along Arcmor Avenue, then Fifth Street South Road, onto Monrose Road. Then they follow Monrose east to Willow Road. Following Willow Road north onto Oak Street, which they follow east to Lance's Mercenary Docks Ward. In the ward they ride to 4th Street, Blue Dove Guild barracks.

Raster isn't much company, though she is diplomatic when she does talk. Bloodgrue for his part speaks little, as he endures the discomfort of riding the first few days. Eventually gathering skill and ease with riding, Bloodgrue gains some comfort on Buttercup by the time they arrive at 4ᵗʰ Street.

Summer 68 Raccoon,

It is evening of the day, after evening meal for most, as Bloodgrue dismounts with less discomfort. The clear sphere above admits little obstacle to the zephyr that creeps slightly through the air on this very hot day.

Sweat trickles off Bloodgrue as he approaches Raster. "Well, besides the mosquitoes and flies, no one harassed us and you are here. That took eight days Master Raster. So eight Dyns please and I will be off … If I can walk?"

Raster clasps arms with Bloodgrue from the back of her horse. She then jumps down and from her coin pouch gives Bloodgrue eight Dyns and two dusters. "Also, there is a small tip for your timely work, apprentice. Thank you Bloodgrue."

Bloodgrue accepts the coins and places them in his pouch. Having completed the job, he departs, to head back towards 4212 Willow Road.

Getting out to Fights Way Avenue, Bloodgrue spots the Mighty Inn and he looks up at the two gods. Judging time, Bloodgrue decides it's time to spend the night.

Entering Mighty Inn at 17 Fights Way, he looks around for the innkeeper.

Finding Innkeeper Harper Soul, Bloodgrue addresses the jalmal. "Gods-grace and good fate master, how much for a night, a meal and a hot bath?"

Harper Soul looks Bloodgrue over, appraising him then nods approvingly. "You've been here before and were good. I'll do it all for two Dyns."

Bloodgrue eagerly extracts two Dyns from his coin pouch and handing them to Harper Soul, Bloodgrue says. "I am Apprentice Dragoman Bloodgrue of 4212 Willow Road, North Docks District. If you have need of dragoman services, I am available until gods-rise. Then I am headed back to Sterric Ward."

Bloodgrue enjoys the steaming hot meal and relaxing hot bath. Bloodgrue eats the hot meal with great abandon, then soaks in the tub, he settles in as he is tired and his muscles and bones ache, thus feeding his body and spirit for the night.

The sleep is deep, when Bloodgrue wakes, he is well rested and it is later in the morning than he usually wakes. Lazily getting ready, Bloodgrue leaves the Mighty Inn behind for 4212 Willow Road.

Summer 71 Raccoon,

It is just noon as Bloodgrue searches the residence for Onar, but the elder dragoman is not to be found.

Bloodgrue leaves eight Dyns on Onar's desk and leaves 4212 Willow Road to go to Teptun Square & Market.

Arriving at the market four hours later, Bloodgrue wanders straight to stall 74. Where Bloodgrue says, "Blue Hair, we have an arrangement we agreed to, so I am here to fulfil my part of the bargain. I owe you nine dusters. As that is ten percent of the pay I received from the job you handed me. She paid eight Dyns dragoman fee and two dusters tip. So I owe eight and a bit. Thus nine coins."

Bloodgrue gives Blue Hair nine dusters and smiling he says eagerly. "Thank you. That was a decent one. She was loaded with coin going to her market and we transported a small fortune in weapons to Lance's."

Bloodgrue spends an hour with Blue Hair discussing the trip and horse riding, then he heads home.

Bloodgrue arrives back at 4212 Willow Road, half-an-hour before gods-set. Bloodgrue finds Onar cleaning up after his evening meal.

Onar nods and dishes Bloodgrue a plate of food. "Sit apprentice and eat. You look exhausted. Stay home tomorrow. We will do lessons."

Bloodgrue nearly melts into his chair and begins to eat the cold meal. "Master, I learnt the basics of horse riding on this job. Eight days of riding a hose with a client. I put the eight Dyns on your desk this afternoon."

"Yes, I found them. Good work Bloodgrue. I want you to go to the weavers in three days. She is getting a new shipment of flax thread. I want some supplies."

"Yes master." Says a tired Bloodgrue; looking forward to a day of rest.

To be continued …

In the next episode 22, *'Bloodgrue's Bedding'*,

Bloodgrue runs an errand for Onar, finding a bonus for himself in extreme conditions over time.

Awesome! You finished an episode of '*Bloodgrue*'.

Let us know what you think of it by going to this this link: www.inupress.ca While you are there, you can join the Inevitable Unicorn Press e-mail subscription list to receive news and updates about work from our authors such as; Rusty Knight, Brian Hill and Aria. When you sign up for the e-mail list, you will receive one free pdf. This free pdf changes with time. In February 2016 the gift was a copy of Rusty Knight's biography of the protagonists, the Black Swans, from his novel, *'Laret'*. Later in 2016, the bonus was an episode from the serial series, *'Lanis'*.

While on the home page of InUPress.ca leave a comment or review telling us what you think of our author's work or your thoughts about the website. We appreciate your time and we will respond to your questions and comments.

Thank you for reading.
Yours,
Rusty Knight of Inevitable Unicorn Press.
www.inupress.ca

Bloodgrue

Fare where?

Rusty Knight

Episode 22, Bloodgrue's Bedding

Bloodgrue
Volume 4: Attractions

Welcome to our serial stories!

If you're not familiar with our serials, think of them as a favorite nighttime program that continues with a new episode each week, only this is in a print format. These are stories that don't necessarily have an end planned for them, or if they do, it's a long way off unlike many television series that we get interested in, only to have them go off air.

Serial stories are a great way to keep you entertained and on edge waiting to see what will happen next, in short enough episodes to enjoy on a lunch break, or before going to bed. Although our stories are designed to be read one episode per week, unlike TV stories, if you just can't wait for the next episode, you can get another one any time.

Be sure to download when you purchase!

It is a good idea to download the episode when you first purchase them. Then, read them at your leisure.

Please feel free to let us know what you think of our serial stories. It's a trend that may take some getting used to, but we've had positive feedback in the past with them.

Now, it's time to enjoy!

From Rusty Knight & InUPress, Thank you

We would like to acknowledge the following for their work in the production of this series.

Our cover design is by, C S Burgar

All of our editing is by, Donna Shumaker (Aria)

Previously *on Bloodgrue* **Summer 60 Raccoon,**

Bloodgrue went to Teptun Square & Market in search of a client. Blue Hair gave Bloodgrue a freight client. A mercenary guild quartermaster, the woman was in search of long-swords. The trip took over nine days long for Bloodgrue, escorting Raster safely for eight of those days, another day after returning her to Lance's Mercenary ward.

In U Press

Inevitable Unicorn Press

Bloodgrue
By Rusty Knight
Episode twenty-two, 'Bloodgrue's Bedding'

In U Press

Inevitable Unicorn Press

We continue on …

Summer 74 Raccoon,

In the darkness of his room Bloodgrue ponders his new quest. The heat in here has Bloodgrue wondering if he should take two water-skins today on this journey south. Onar's list isn't large and the pouch he is sending is light, so two skins won't slow Bloodgrue down much. He gets out of his bed and using his chamber pot he plans further.

Summer 76 Raccoon,

Draining the second water-skin as he steps up to 3226 Chase Street. Bloodgrue brushes the sweat off his face and arms. His tunic is running with sweat. Looking up into the clear sphere Bloodgrue is glad he brought two skins with him. He's filled them both twice today. Without them he wouldn't have been able to travel. The gods breathe properly, east and moderately. But it's not enough in this heat to keep a man, or boy, cool. Still thirsty, Bloodgrue enters Bareington Tailors, looking to find the man he was sent to talk with.

Inside, the shade it is much cooler than outdoors, but even in here the staff members sweat profusely.

Bloodgrue spots a toymal of about thirty years of age. Speaking in toy as he approaches the man. Bloodgrue asks. "Excuse me; I am looking for Master Popalma. Are you him?"

The mature toymal looks up indifferently at Bloodgrue. He addresses Bloodgrue politely. "Gods-grace and good fate, yes I am Tailor Popalma. How may I help you?"

Bloodgrue heaves a sigh. Bloodgrue thinks, '*Easy enough right?*'. He says, "Gods-grace and good fate Master Tailor Popalma. I am Apprentice Dragoman Bloodgrue of 4212 Willow Road. I come seeking goods for my Master, Master Dragoman Onar. Do you have a moment to sell me some goods?"

For some reason this greatly cheers up Popalma. He stands and walks close to Bloodgrue to clasp arms. "Dragoman Bloodgrue, if you do me a favour and courier a parcel today, I will spend all the time you want when you return."

Bloodgrue grins eagerly. He is out on an errand and gets a courier job. What could be better? "Of course master, it is my work that I do. What and where is it going?"

Popalma walks over to a bench and retrieves a larger parcel. Handing it to Bloodgrue, Bloodgrue estimates it to be twenty pounds, not bad if he straps it to his back.

Popalma answers. "This goes to 2012 Marr Street, Lander's Ward, to a Master Bearis Mon. Please deliver it as soon as possible, Dragoman Bloodgrue."

Bloodgrue nods. "If I could fill both my waterskins from your well, I will be on my way. I should be back in two or three days."

Popalma nods and points to a large barrel. "Please, feel free to fill your skins from there."

Bloodgrue fills both skins from the tap on the barrel. Then mounting the parcel to his pack on his back, and secures his two skins. He grudgingly heads out into the heat again.

Summer 77 Raccoon,

The house is smallish and devoid of embellishments. Bloodgrue knocks on the door again. With it being well past noon, Bloodgrue wonders if the master is home.

Finally, an ancient jalmal opens the door. Bloodgrue in trade jal greets him. "Gods-grace and good fate Master Bearis Mon. I bring a delivery from Bareington Tailor's."

The old jal cups a hand behind his ear and squeaks out. "Speak up, the gods are roaring in my ears. What did you say?"

Bloodgrue holds up his hand while smiling. He takes the package off his back and points to it then into the house.

Bearis Mon nods and waves Bloodgrue inside his home.

Entering, Bloodgrue looks to the common room table and cheerfully sets the package on the wooden structure. He takes out the parchment leaf from his belt pouch and the carbon stick.

Placing the parchment leaf on the table, he points to the space set aside for the mark, Bloodgrue offers Bearis Mon the carbon stick.

The old man sighs, and instead opens the parcel. Inside he exposes a new, heavy wool cloak, trimmed with sheep skin.

Bearis Mon tries on the cloak, it fits him perfectly coming to just two inches from the floor, hanging freely around him comfortably, closing around in front.

Bearis Mon nods smiling and reaches for the carbon stick, taking it he makes his mark in the space available.

Bloodgrue stashes the parchment and carbon stick in his belt pouch and clasps arms with Bearis Mon. Leaving the house, he heads for the tailor's shop.

Summer 78 Raccoon,

Staggering again as he nears Bareington Tailors, Bloodgrue has fought the breath of the gods today. They must be well over one-hundred kilometres-an-hours, pushing him along Chase Avenue. While on Fifth Street South Road he struggled, adding at least twenty minutes to the journey.

Entering 3226 Chase Avenue, well before noon, Bloodgrue finds Popalma busy weaving flannel sheets. The toymal looks over as Bloodgrue enters the tailor shop, and he stops work. Popalma stands and walks over to greet Bloodgrue. "Gods-grace and good fate dragoman Bloodgrue. Thank you for your work. How did it go?"

Bloodgrue smiles and opening his belt pouch he retrieves the parchment and carbon stick. Handing them to Popalma they clasp arms after the Tailor confirms the mark.

"Ok, so you came to me for business. Let us do business, dragoman. What is it you seek?" asks a professional Popalma.

Bloodgrue, tired from fighting to stay standing in the wind, decides not to test his memory. He withdraws Onar's vellum list from his belt pouch. Looking over the fourth line toydon script that he was schooled in, he reads it to himself to familiarize him.

Then lowering the list, Bloodgrue begins. "The first thing my master wants is a set of clothing shears. A sturdy set he can work with."

Popalma nods and retrieves a box of scissors and shears then choosing a set he offers it to Bloodgrue. "You can take these to your master for fifteen Dyns."

Bloodgrue, not to certain on the qualities to be looking for, looks over the shears. Then he offers. "I will take then to my master for five Dyns, they seem light."

Popalma seeing Bloodgrue knows little about shears, in the way he is handling them, stands his ground. "Dragoman, those are decent sturdy shears. I must insist on fifteen Dyns for them."

Bloodgrue sees no opportunity for betterment here. He is hoping to catch a better price on other items. He answers. "I will agree; I'll take these for fifteen Dyns. I also need two sewing needles."

Popalma, assuming the list is long, desires to move along on the small items. "Okay, two needles for seven dusters each, so give me fourteen dusters and they are yours."

Bloodgrue, feeling this is good, nods. "Also, my master wants ten spools of black thread. Good flax thread, not the light stuff." Bloodgrue is now in territory he knows and can assess better.

Popalma, having used most of his thread already, has limited supply so he asks. "I would like nine dusters per spool and ten is all I can spare of the black."

Bloodgrue finds this high for flax thread. "I think you are being overzealous on the pricing, how about eight dusters. I will go that high as it is my master's coins."

Popalma, seeing Bloodgrue seems to know a bit about the items, accepts this. "Okay I'll accept eight but only ten spools sold."

Bloodgrue nods and looks at his list again. There are two more items on the list. "Okay he wants ten spools of red flannel thread."

Popalma having even less red flannel thread goes for more. "Okay, I tell you my flannel is running low and I have work to finish with it. I will sell you ten spools for thirteen dusters each, it's not negotiable, apprentice."

Bloodgrue, noting this was the one item Onar insisted on getting, decides to not fight the issue. "Okay, but what about ten of orange as well? That is Onar's last item on his list."

Popalma hesitates. Then he adds the black thread and red thread from his stock to the shears and needles for Bloodgrue. He looks at his last four spools of Imvor-Orange thread. "I will sell you three at fourteen dusters each."

Bloodgrue, seeing this as robbery and seeing he has already been robbed, refuses this pricing. "No, that's indecent pricing. You got too much for the red already. I will pay ten for the orange."

Popalma looks at Bloodgrue while saying. "Not less than fourteen."

Bloodgrue, hoping for at least one spool for less, continues. "Okay, tell you what, I will buy whatever you will sell at the same price as the red."

Popalma shakes his head vigorously. "No … Fourteen … But I don't have enough, so no, I'm not selling any orange … Unless you pay fifteen."

Bloodgrue balks at this theft. "Not likely Master Popalma. We are done shopping for my master. I will pay that up if you will bundle it up."

Popalma puts all the goods in a small canvas sack as Bloodgrue pays out all of Onar's coins except twenty-six dusters. The two clasp arms after the exchange is made. Bloodgrue puts the sack in his backpack then sits near Popalma again.

Bloodgrue continues, saying, "My good tailor, my coin purse has a few coins I can part with as well. But please, be kinder to me. I work harder for my coins then my master workers for his."

Bloodgrue feels a little thirsty after being out in the wind all morning. "May I fill my skins from your barrel again? I'll pay a duster each."

Popalma frowns, smirking, he then says to Bloodgrue. "Fill your skins. No cost, as you are buying from me. We will see what you are buying, how easy I go."

Bloodgrue fills both skins. After drinking he sits again.

"I think, first thing I seek is a feather pillow. Mine is sad, it wants a companion." speaks Bloodgrue energetically.

Popalma fetches a decent feather pillow. Handing it to Bloodgrue, he asks. "I want twelve dusters Bloodgrue."

Bloodgrue knows they typically sell for twenty, so isn't going to haggle over this one. He places the pillow on the bench to begin the pile.

"Okay, I too need sewing needles." asks Bloodgrue.

Popalma offers Bloodgrue. "I have two left, for fifteen dusters each."

Bloodgrue recalls Onar's cost of seven, so he counters; giving way that these might be Popalma's last ones. "Sorry, but that is way too much. I will buy them for eight, maybe."

Popalma, seeing perhaps he was too exuberant in his opening requests. "Okay, maybe not fifteen, but certainly not eight. Let's say twelve each."

Bloodgrue wonders what haggling over two sewing needles will achieve over all on his list, he decides. "I accept."

Popalma adds his two needles onto the bench.

Bloodgrue sighs and looks at the box of shears and scissors. Seeing a smaller pair that he likes, he picks them out and hands them to Popalma. "I want these as well."

Popalma wonders why Bloodgrue wants the scissors, but opens with. "You can have these scissor for eight Dyns, apprentice."

Bloodgrue wonders if he can get a better deal. "How about … seventy-two dusters for those?"

Popalma, knowing he is giving Bloodgrue a fair deal already, answers. "No … I want eight Dyns."

Bloodgrue tries to see if he can budge Popalma. "I can afford seven. I will have to leave them here."

Popalma decides to part with the scissors. "I will let you have them for seventy-four dusters but no less, dragoman."

They add these to the pile as Bloodgrue nods in agreement. "I will take them. I need five spools of red wool thread, though."

Popalma, seeing his thread is too low to really be selling more, offers Bloodgrue. "I will sell you three spools at eight dusters each."

Bloodgrue frowns and counters. "I won't be able to match them later and I need five. So no. I will pay seven if I can only get three spools."

Popalma looks at Bloodgrue in consternation. "Look, my thread is low and I need it for my work. My apprentice is working her fingers and feet off spinning thread for four weavers and tailors. I can't be just selling it off cheap. I want eight, if I sell it."

Bloodgrue, seeing it is futile trying to get a lower price, motions to add the thread.

"I would like four flannel sheets as well. What colour and what price for matched pairs?"

Popalma smiles eagerly. "I can sell you two match pairs of blue flannel flat sheets. I am asking forty-eight dusters per sheet."

Bloodgrue frowns, "I would like to see them first."

Popalma shows Bloodgrue four matched blue flannel sheets. Bloodgrue examines them finding them average quality.

"I offer you forty-two dusters each. They are of average quality."

Popalma, seeing Bloodgrue examine and understand the quality of the flannel, agrees. They place the sheets with the other items while Bloodgrue adds. "I also seek two pillowcases."

Popalma brings Bloodgrue two pillowcases to match the sheets. Bloodgrue inspects these, finding flaws in the one, he asks. "How much?"

Popalma opens his haggling with. "Twelve dusters each, I am asking."

Bloodgrue, wanting matching pillowcases for his sheets and knowing the one is pretty good but one is flawed, is getting tired of this. He decides. "Okay you are being reasonable at twelve. I'll take them."

The pillowcases are added to the collection.

As Bloodgrue is counting the coins to pay, a colourful orange and red patterned mat catches his eye.

He points to the mat. "How much for the mat?"

Popalma proudly hands the mat to Bloodgrue to be examined.

Bloodgrue is very impressed with the craftsmanship in the weaving. It is extremely well done.

Popalma looks at Bloodgrue and he says. "I like you, I wanted twenty-five but I will ask you for twenty-three Dyns."

Bloodgrue can't resist trying for one more deal, so he counters with. "I will take it for twenty-one right now, no further asking for deals."

Popalma frowns, sighing he clasps arms with Bloodgrue. "Deal dragoman, we can do that. Is there any more, or can I return to making more items for my customers, that pay me?" He winks as he clasps arms.

Bloodgrue pays Popalma and leaves three dusters extra tip.

Their business completed Bloodgrue carefully packs all the items. Wrapping the pillow after rolling it up, he ties it under his backpack. Saying a last farewell, Bloodgrue departs and heads for 4212 Willow Road.

Summer 80 Raccoon,

Entering 4212 Willow Road, near evening meal time, with his load settled on him comfortably, Bloodgrue ponders why, when he is home the gods breathe random wrong directions. Like they are telling him they are going to alter his life.

Bloodgrue finds Onar in the kitchen preparing evening meal.

"Master, I have your things, except the orange thread. I also found a job while I was out, earning two Dyns. I will put your things in your office."

Onar mutters disjointedly, and then he speaks up loudly. "Thank you apprentice … You are going to Lexigrapher Steirn tomorrow. She requested you."

"Thank you master." says Bloodgrue weakly.

Bloodgrue goes to his room, unpacks and takes Onar's things to his room, leaving two Dyns on the desk.

Returning to his room, Bloodgrue puts a pair of new sheets on his bed. Putting away the other items, he returns to the kitchen and serves himself leftovers from Onar's meal.

Then Bloodgrue goes to bed.

To be continued …

In the next episode twenty-three, *'Fourth Line Script'*

Bloodgrue is summoned by a Lexigrapher, fearing a menial job, the dragoman finds this is far from menial and is put on a series of tasks by Lexigrapher Steirn. Including a stint into Western Madison.

Awesome! You finished an episode of '*Bloodgrue*'.

Let us know what you think of it by going to this this link: www.inupress.ca While you are there, you can join the Inevitable Unicorn Press e-mail subscription list to receive news and updates about work from our authors such as; Rusty Knight, Brian Hill and Aria. When you sign up for the e-mail list, you will receive one free pdf. This free pdf changes with time. In February 2016 the gift was a copy of Rusty Knight's biography of the protagonists, the Black Swans, from his novel, *'Laret'*. Later in 2016, the bonus was an episode from the serial series, *'Lanis'*.

While on the home page of InUPress.ca leave a comment or review telling us what you think of our author's work, or your thoughts about the website. We appreciate your time and we will respond to your questions and comments.

Thank you for reading.
Yours,
Rusty Knight of Inevitable Unicorn Press.
www.inupress.ca

Bloodgrue
Volume 4: Attractions

As producer at InUPress.ca and author of the Bloodgrue serial short-story series, I thank you for reading Bloodgrue Volume 4: Attractions by Rusty Knight.

The series is to be continued with Bloodgrue Volume 5: Rulings.

These will be found at InUPress.ca and Amazon and Kobo.

Previous books in the series are now available at Amazon:

Bloodgrue Volume 1: Fare Where!

Bloodgrue Volume 2: Breaths

Bloodgrue Volume 3: Business also available on Kobo and InUPress.ca

Bloodgrue Volume 4: Attractions also available on InUPress.ca and Kobo also

As producer at InUPress.ca and author of the Bloodgrue, Markus and Lanis serial short-story series, I thank you for reading the series.

Yours,

Rusty Knight and InUPress.ca.

Dalan e-zine can also be found on InUPress.ca as well other works can be found at InUPress.ca, Amazon, Kobo, Goodreads, Niume and Scriggler.

Books in the Bloodgrue series now available at www.inupress.ca, Kindle, Kobo, as well as on Amazon as paperback:

Bloodgrue Volume 1: Fare Where? Amazon and Kindle only

Bloodgrue Volume 2: Breaths Amazon and Kindle only

Bloodgrue Volume 3: Business

Bloodgrue Volume 4: Attractions

www.ingramcontent.com/pod-product-compliance
Lightning Source LLC
Chambersburg PA
CBHW041025170626

46815CB00001B/10